The DARK POOL

In the President's Service: Episode 2

ACE COLLINS

Elk Lake Publishing
The Dark Pool: In the President's Service, Episode Two

Copyright © 2014 by Ace Collins
Requests for information should be addressed to:
Elk Lake Publishing, Atlanta, GA 30024

Create Space ISBN-13 NUMBER: 978-1-942513-15-5

Cover and graphics design: Stephanie Chontos and Anna O'Brien
Editing: Kathy Ide
Cover Model: Alison Johnson
Other images via: *www.dollarphotoclub.com*
Photography: Ace Collins
Published in association with Joyce Hart Agent Hartline Literary Agency.

To Alison

CHAPTER 1

Monday, March 16, 1942
10:45 PM

The man's arms moved in piston-like fashion as he raced across an open field. Though he was tall and ruggedly built, his rapidly beating heart rumbled like a kettledrum and his lungs felt as though they were being yanked through his chest. The bitter-cold March wind tore into his face, causing his cheekbones to all but cut through his skin. Yet, in spite of his mind pleading with him to stop, he kept going. He had to run. He had no choice. It was either get away or die.

Glancing over his left shoulder into the night, he noted four figures with flashlights moving toward him. Were they getting closer? He thought so, but perhaps fatigue was just playing games with him. After all, he'd been sprinting for at least a mile.

His need to flee was almost overruled by a longing to slow down—maybe even give up. But he couldn't do that. Death was

ACE COLLINS

better than going back into the hole. So he kept his legs moving across the flat prairie landscape. Even if his heart burst and he instantly fell dead, that would be better than the fate that awaited him back there.

Up ahead, he saw headlights moving from left to right. A highway! If he could get to it, maybe someone would pick him up. Then the monsters chasing him couldn't drag him back and continue beating him or filling his body with more of the mind-numbing drugs.

The hope of escape from his pursuers enabled him to push himself even harder. As he got to within half a mile of the road, he saw more cars. Sweet freedom was almost in his grasp!

His breath ragged, his chest heaving, he felt more like an old plow horse than a sleek thoroughbred. But victory would not be earned by the contestant with the best form. No, the blue ribbon was reserved for those who had the heart to battle until they broke the tape. And tonight he was going to give everything within himself to achieve his goal.

In the dim light offered by the sliver of moon, he didn't notice the pool of shallow water until it splashed up into his face. And then it was too late. He lost his balance and fell forward into the mud. Pushing his torso up, he glanced back. His pursuers were closing fast.

Fighting tears of anger and disappointment, he rose to his feet. Soaked, cold, and exhausted, he glanced at the highway. So close but still out of reach.

When he turned back, the four men who'd been chasing him stood close enough he could see the whites of their eyes in the dark night. He could also make out the rifles in their hands.

"Go ahead and shoot me," he growled. "Put me out of my misery."

The quartet stopped at the edge of the pool. They said nothing. He knew they wouldn't.

A tall man walked up beside them. "Go get him," he ordered. "But don't beat him. We need him healthy and in one piece."

As the four mute warriors waded toward him, the defeated runner fell into the mud and wept.

CHAPTER 2

Monday, March 16, 1942
11:05 PM
Ithaca, New York

Helen Meeker turned her gaze from President Roosevelt back to Reggie Fister. It seemed during times of war doing the right thing for your country often meant going against every emotion in your heart. By shooting this man, had she sealed a death sentence for her partner and the sister she barely knew? And would she be able to live with herself if those two special people died thanks to her seemingly rash decision? With the clock ticking and both Reese and Alison in the hands of Fister's unknown confederates, she sensed that question would haunt her the rest of her life.

She turned her attention from FDR to the room's main door when six more Secret Service agents rushed in with guns drawn. It had taken them long enough. She'd pulled the trigger of her

Colt more than two minutes ago.

To these trained professionals, the scene must have looked like something out of a poorly scripted B movie. The smell of gunpowder hovered in the air, and two men lay bleeding on the floor. Yet in the face of all the violence and chaos, the leaders of the free world seemed calm. Roosevelt leaned back in his chair, lighting a cigarette, while Churchill scowled like an angry bulldog at the wounded and bleeding man on the carpet.

Secret Service agent Clay Barnes jerked the onetime British army hero off the floor and shoved him into a wooden chair. After handcuffing the man's left wrist to the arm of the antique, he turned toward the other agents. "Get the doc."

One agent left, but the others stood there with perplexed expressions.

"The fun is over, so you can put those guns away. Helen seems to have the situation well under control."

Before Meeker had a chance to even blush, the White House physician rushed onto the scene. He charged past the agents like an Olympic sprinter headed toward the finish line.

"What have we got here?" he asked breathlessly, medical bag in hand.

Meeker knew the dry-witted doctor well. A gray-haired, short, blocky man in his fifties, Cleveland Mills had been the head surgeon at New York Mercy before being asked to look after the president and his staff. Now the father of three served as a fourth in bridge more often than as a medical caregiver. But at the moment, his top-notch skills were needed, and he seemed eager to knock off the rust and use them.

"The hero turned out to be a louse," Barnes explained, pointing to Fister. "But he needs some medical care before we haul him off to a jail cell."

"What about that man?" Mills gestured toward Nigel Andrews.

"The British scoundrel shot him." The agent soberly shook his head. "Probably dead before he hit the floor."

The doctor rubbed his chin. "Well, if you're sure the living one is properly restrained, I'll take a look."

Barnes scoffed. "If he tries to run away, he'll be dragging a heavy, century-old chair with him."

After collapsing onto the couch in exhaustion, Meeker watched the White House doctor examine the wrist she'd shot. Though she had no medical training, she'd seen several injuries like Fister's and knew his wasn't fatal. After all, she hadn't intended to kill him, just render him harmless.

Still, she doubted his wound would heal completely before he faced the gallows. In times of war, justice was dealt out quickly and with no mercy. Still, unless she worked some kind of miracle, Fister probably had more time to draw breath than Alison or Reese did. The innocent were not favored over the guilty in the game of life.

Though anxious to begin her search for her sister and partner, Meeker felt obligated to hold her position until this matter was fully cleared up.

Her eyes glued on the doctor's efforts to clean and dress Fister's wound, she heard the British leader whispering to her boss.

"We can't let this little drama leak to the press. If newspapers in the UK or the US reported that a British hero tried to kill me, that would upset everything we English stand for."

"It wouldn't look good for a war hero to be exposed as a Nazi spy either," the president replied flatly. He took a long draw from his cigarette holder. "Besides, neither one of us is supposed to be on an estate in New York. As far as the world is concerned, I'm in Washington and you're in London. We can't blow this cover. So what story do you suggest?"

Churchill shrugged. "I'm certain my people can come up with a reason for Colonel Fister to disappear. Perhaps a plane crash or some such thing. And Corporal Andrews could be on the same flight." He looked at Nigel and shook his head. "Shame about the lad. He saved our lives."

FDR nodded. "Helen gets a large part of the credit for that too. After all, if she hadn't shot your hero, our wives would be planning our funerals."

Pretending to ignore the chatter, Meeker kept her eyes on Nigel Andrews's still body. His precious Becky would never see him again. And the cause of his death would be forever masked in a lie. Andrews had put his life on the line for his country. But no one would ever know.

"Wonder if we'll ever find out what really happened," Roosevelt mused.

The British leader sighed. "I doubt it. Colonel Fister talked my ear off as we drove up here, but I'm sure he'll clam up now."

As Meeker awaited the president's response, she thought she saw Andrews's right hand twitch. Could Fister's shot have missed its mark?

She hurried across the room, bent over the fallen Brit, and grabbed his wrist. She felt a faint pulse.

"Doctor," she yelled, "Andrews is still alive!"

The physician looked up from his work. "Finish wrapping this up," he barked to a Secret Service man. After handing him a roll of gauze, Mills picked up his bag and rushed to the man he'd been assured was dead. After a quick examination, he ordered, "Get him on the couch."

Two agents who had been waiting for something to do lifted Andrews to the spot where Meeker had been sitting a few minutes before. The doctor ripped open his jacket and shirt and examined the chest wound. Andrews's eyes fluttered and opened.

His gaze locked onto Meeker. "Are Churchill and Roosevelt all right?" he croaked out.

"They're fine," Meeker assured him. "And we got Fister."

Andrews breathed a sigh and closed his eyes. "I'm not a spy. I couldn't turn on Great Britain."

"Everyone knows that now."

The doctor turned back to the agents. "We need to transport this man to the nearest hospital. Have you got a wagon?"

Barnes nodded. "We always have an ambulance on call. It's behind the house. What about Fister?"

Mills shook his head. "Just have your man finish wrapping that wrist. His wound is nothing a prison doc can't handle."

As the physician went back to cleaning the gunshot wound, Andrews lifted his head. "I need to talk to Miss Meeker."

"You need to rest, son," Mills advised. "You've lost a lot of blood. You could fog out on us at any moment. Save your talking till later."

"No," Andrews hissed. "A man's life is on the line."

The doctor peered at Meeker. "You can listen to what he has to say, but don't get in my way."

"Yes, sir." She knelt beside the couch and leaned close to the injured man's ear.

"Find The Lord's Rest," Andrews whispered, his voice faint but steady.

"I did. It's an old house in Jerusalem, New York. I've been there."

"Good." He sighed. "So you got him away from them."

"Got who away from whom?"

"The FBI agent."

"Henry Reese?"

"Yes. I heard two guys say they were taking him to The Lord's Rest."

A cold chill ran down Meeker's spine. She'd set that place on fire when she rescued the Shellmeyer girl. If Henry was in there, he would have been burned alive.

She drew closer to the Brit's face. "When did they grab Henry?"

"Just before dawn."

"Where?"

"Just outside of Elmira. I had a flat tire and Reese caught up with me. Before I could tell him my story, a car pulled up, and two men jumped out and started shooting."

Andrews took three shallow gasps before continuing. "I ran

off. Hid in the woods. When Reese ran out of ammunition, they knocked him out and threw him into their vehicle. That's when I heard them talking about where they were going."

Meeker's heart lurched. Elmira was close enough to The Lord's Rest that they probably got Reese there before she arrived and torched the place. She hadn't checked all of the rooms before she found the girl. Had she left her partner to die in that fire? The thought chilled her to the bone.

Andrews's breathing became more labored. The doctor shot Meeker a warning glare. But she had to get as many answers as she could.

"Were the men who got Henry German agents? Did one of them have a tattoo just above his hand?"

Andrews's eyes closed as he slipped out of consciousness.

Meeker gasped. "Is he—?"

He'll be fine," the doctor assured her. "But I don't expect he'll wake before tomorrow night."

That wasn't soon enough. Vaulting to her feet, Meeker whirled around and glared at Reggie Fister.

He grinned at her. "What's wrong, Helen? You look as though you've seen a ghost."

Meeker marched across the room to the recently unmasked enemy spy. "What do you know about The Lord's Rest?" she demanded.

"I have no idea what you're talking about." He shrugged. "Sounds like a funeral home to me, which is most likely where Reese should be. Let me know when the services are and I'll send flowers."

Meeker drew back her arm and brought her palm and fingers full force against Fister's cheek. To her deep disappointment, he didn't even flinch.

"My, don't we have a temper?" He raised an eyebrow at her. "You certainly didn't act this way when I held you in my arms and whispered those tempting lies in your ears."

Blood rushed to Meeker's cheeks.

Fister chuckled. "That's right. You were just part of the assignment. My job was to shift your attention. So I fed you lines to get your focus off the case. And you wanted me. I saw it in your eyes and heard it in your voice. One more romantic night and I would've had you."

"You're disgusting," she spat. "And if anything happens to Henry or Alison, I will make sure you pay!"

Fister winked. "I look forward to you trying to do that."

Her heart pounding, Meeker bit her tongue and moved back to where Barnes stood. She grabbed his arm and yanked him out into the hall, where Fister couldn't overhear her. "We don't have much time if we're going to save my sister."

"And Reese."

Meeker choked back a sob. "I'm afraid we might be too late to save Henry."

The Secret Service agent crossed his arms. "What do you mean?"

"I need you to check out a house that burned down earlier today just outside Jerusalem, New York. It's called The Lord's Rest. You'll find at least two bodies in the ashes: men who were working with the Germans and likely Fister. But you may find a third one too.

"Henry?"

"Get an FBI team up there as soon as possible. Take control of that crime scene and dig through every piece of debris."

The agent nodded. "As soon as the phones come back up, I'll take care of it." He smiled. "But I'll bet we don't find Henry in the rubble. He's a pretty crafty guy. He can get out of pretty much anything."

"I hope you're right," she replied softly.

"You need anything else?"

"Yeah. Keep after Fister until he breaks. Pound him and pound him, and don't let him sleep. Anything he says, no matter how insignificant it might seem, write it down."

"What if he doesn't break before the deadline? He said if he wasn't at the pickup site before ten o'clock on Friday night, both Reese and Alison would be killed."

Meeker groaned. Like she needed to be reminded of that little detail.

"Maybe we should let him keep his appointment. We've made trades in the past for spies."

She rubbed her hands over her arms in an effort to shake a chill. "The government can't let Fister go, even if it meant saving Alison's life. That's not the way things work, and you know it."

Barnes nodded.

"Our only hope is to find my sister—and Reese, if he's still alive—before the deadline. And Friday night will be here all too fast, so you need to get moving."

"You got it." Barnes took off down the hall.

Meeker hoped her old partner would forgive her, but since blood was thicker than water, she was going after her sister first.

CHAPTER 3

Tuesday, March 17, 1942
12:01 PM
Ten miles south of Springfield, Illinois

Fredrick Bauer knocked on the back wall of the sixty-year-old frame barn. As he gazed at the empty horse stall to his right, the hardwood floor in the stall dropped a few inches and slid open. After glancing over his shoulder to make sure he was not being observed, Bauer walked down the steep stairs.

Fifteen steps later he entered a brightly lit twenty-by-sixty-foot chamber that looked more like a laboratory than a cellar. It had taken him five years to design and create this place. A wide variety of testing equipment sat on a half dozen tables. With a full surgical center on the far side and a gun range at the back, he had everything he needed here. Outside of the FBI, this was likely the finest crime lab in the country. That thought brought him a tremendous sense of accomplishment and pride.

The most remarkable facet of this operation was that only a

handful of people knew of its existence.

A woman with high cheekbones and wide shoulders looked up from behind a desk as he crossed the room. She wore dark-framed glasses, a straight black skirt, a simple white blouse, and flats. Her blonde hair was tightly secured in a librarian's bun, and there were no signs of makeup on her pale skin.

Her expression was even more severe and detached than her appearance. If she felt any emotion, she disguised it well.

After closing a file she'd been reading and placing it to one side, she ran her long, thin fingers over her starched collar and stood. Her stance was almost military—two-by-fours were more pliable. Though her eyes studied him, she remained mute, showing she knew her place.

"Emma," Bauer asked, "how is our prisoner?"

"He is fine, sir."

Good. They would be needing him very soon. And he'd have to be in perfect shape.

Bauer strolled past the woman toward a cell in the far wall. This captive was his ace in the hole, the centerpiece of a plan that would finally be put into operation. After pulling a key from his coat pocket, he opened a windowless door and glanced in. The room's tall, ruggedly built guest looked up from his bunk, his eyes glowing in the light.

Emma came up from behind. "Is there something I should know?" she whispered.

Bauer shut and bolted the door. "Our operation last night did not go as planned," he explained.

"What do we do now?"

He walked around Emma and returned to the room's entry. When he arrived at the stairs, he stopped. "The less you know the better. You just make sure our guest stays healthy."

"Yes, sir."

He marched up four steps, then turned. "Once we get all the information we need, a team will come here to prepare him."

"Dr. Snider?"

"Yes, and two others."

Bauer climbed the remaining steps. Once back on the barn's main level, he stepped aside and waited for the secret panel to close. Once it was secure, he walked to one of the building's side doors.

As he stepped out into the sunshine, he looked across the snow-swept landscape. He'd warned Fister that a woman would be his undoing. Thankfully, he'd set a plan in place just in case Helen Meeker figured things out. The meddlesome woman would be busy in Arkansas while Bauer and his team went to work springing Fister from FBI custody. All things considered, this would make for an interesting challenge. Those were good for keeping the mind sharp.

Pushing his hands into his pants pockets, Bauer walked to the century-old farmhouse where Abraham Lincoln had once spent the night. After pouring a cup of tea, he turned his console Zenith radio on, tuned it to a classical music station, and smiled as the sounds of Wagner filled the room. He picked up the copy of *Gone with the Wind* that he'd left on top of the radio, found a dog-eared page, settled into a chair, and escaped into another time and place.

CHAPTER 4

Tuesday, March 17, 1942
2:05 PM
Albany, New York

After the warden at the city jail made sure Fister's right wrist received a second examination, a bit of treatment, and a fresh bandage, he took the spy to a small conference room and handcuffed his left arm to a table. Clay Barnes followed every step of the way.

This was new territory for the tall, dark-haired, thirty-five-year-old Secret Service agent. He wasn't used to either looking after a prisoner or being asked to pull information from him. But with the power and communication issues caused by the storm, Barnes had to fill that role until an FBI agent arrived and took Fister off his hands.

As the cocky and seemingly relaxed Brit settled into a chair, Barnes sat across the small table from him. Crossing his arms, he began his interrogation.

"This will go easier if you just give me the information I need now."

Fister raised an eyebrow. "You know that's not going to happen." His tone was not defiant, but assured and confident. He grinned and leaned back in his chair. "So I guess it's your move."

Two people's lives were on the line. Barnes had to get beyond that smug attitude and make this traitor uncomfortable enough to talk.

"Okay, Reggie … Can I call you Reggie?"

"Fine with me."

"Well, Reggie, here's what's going to happen. I'm going to pester you with questions. Incessantly. You're not going to eat, sleep, or even lie down. You won't be allowed to go to the bathroom without a guard at your side. Those handcuffs will start chafing. You'll get drowsy. Your muscles will beg for fuel, and your mind will start to fog over. You'll begin to want sleep more than anything in the world." Barnes lifted his bushy eyebrows. "No one can hold out forever. Even the strongest man breaks at some point."

"But I'm not a normal man," Fister bragged. "That's why I have this job. My skin is thick, my will strong, and my brain sharp. But, if it helps you pass time, you may go on with your lecture."

Barnes ignored the taunt. He looked the prisoner in the eye and leaned forward over the table. "Just for sport, I'll make the first question an easy one. Where is Alison?"

"Which Alison?" Fister shot back. "I've known a number of Alisons. There was a lovely blonde in Dublin, with the voice of a meadowlark and the morals of an alley cat. Then there was Alison in Paris. She was dark and sultry, and she loved my accent."

Taking a deep breath, Barnes forced a smile. "If you're so smart, I shouldn't have to explain which Alison I'm interested in."

Fister grinned. "If you mean Helen's sister, I don't know where she is. I've never even met her. But I do know we have her. And Henry Reese too."

"So where are they?"

Fister laughed. "All you have to do to save them is let me go." He shrugged. "Two for one sounds like a pretty good deal to me."

Barnes slammed his right fist on the metal table so hard that the dull ringing echoed for several seconds. "I can get tough if I need to. I could bring my fist down on the back of your head and drive your nose into that table, and I would enjoy it thoroughly."

The thought of working over the handsome face of this traitor appealed to Barnes more than he wanted to admit. In fact, the only thing keeping him from beating the man to death was his professional resolve and his personal faith. As the son of a Methodist preacher, he couldn't allow his burning rage for this individual to dictate his actions. If he did, he would never be able to face his father again.

But he couldn't let Fister know that. He had to convince him that he would break his neck on a moment's notice.

25

A flicker outside the window drew Barnes to cross the room. The clouds had lifted, and lights glowed in the buildings below. The phones would probably be working again within hours. That meant Fister would soon be the FBI's problem. And they wouldn't just ask a few questions. With one of their own having been kidnapped, their interrogation would get ugly.

Turning to face the prisoner, Barnes dropped his arms to his side and slid his hands into his trouser pockets. "So you put into motion a plan that included killing the free world's greatest leaders, but you don't even know what happened to the two people who got kidnapped?"

"Who said I put the plan in motion?" Fister shot back. "I just knew about it." His drumming fingers on the table caused the handcuffs to rattle on the surface. "Do you think I'm the brains here? I don't call the shots."

"Then who does?"

"Someone I've never met. I'm just a player in all this. I have no more power than you do. We both just do what we're told. The difference is, this game is fun for me. I enjoy playing with people's hearts and lives."

Barnes pointed his index finger at the prisoner. "You honestly expect me to believe that you're powerless?"

Fister shrugged. "You believed I was a hero, didn't you?"

Barnes hated to admit that Fister was right. But everyone had been fooled. They'd all been awed by this handsome man, even bragged to friends and family that they'd met him. But he couldn't give Fister the satisfaction of knowing he'd hoodwinked them.

"My job was to take out Churchill and Roosevelt. I failed. But the people who tell me what to do had a backup plan in place just in case things didn't work.

"How long have you been working for the Nazis?"

Fister looked toward the ceiling. "Isn't there supposed to be a single overhead light shining directly into my eyes?" He leveled his gaze at Barnes. "You're not very good at this, are you?"

"I'm leaving the tried-and-true stuff for the FBI. My approach is different. I'll treat you like a man and not a stray dog, even though placing that label on you would insult a flea-bitten hound."

"Was that supposed to hurt?" Fister laughed, then rested his elbows on the table. "Let me tell you what you should be saying. 'Okay, Reggie, I'm going to get out my knife and slowly peel back the skin from your body. I'll begin at your toes and work my way up to your head. If that doesn't make you talk, I'll fillet you like a trout. But no matter how much pain you're in, I won't let you die.' That's how this game is played. You need to get with the program, Clay."

"Maybe they play that way on your side," Barnes growled. He stood and leaned against the wall. "You want to know how I figured out what side you were playing for?"

"Could be interesting." Fister shrugged. "Besides, you might as well talk, since I'm not going to."

"Reason number one. You were fighting the Nazis in France when your unit was attacked. All of your men escaped. You were left behind, but somehow you weren't killed. The Nazis would've skinned you alive if you'd been captured."

"Interesting. Go on."

"Reason number two. You tried to kill the president and the prime minister, then shot the man who figured it out. The fact that your supposed best friend turned on you speaks volumes."

"Don't forget the part where I turned Helen Meeker's head," Fister cut in. "Have you ever kissed her, Barnes? She's a real good kisser. There's passion burning in that woman. She's like a volcano ready to explode."

Barnes knew the prisoner was trying to get under his skin and cause him to lose focus. He was experienced enough to let the jabs roll off his back and move on. "So clearly, you were working for the Germans."

Fister blinked. "Really? I don't seem to recall that. You'll have to show me my official Nazi employment records."

Barnes walked back to the table, retook his seat, and leaned toward his guest. "You do know you're going to die, right?"

"So are you," Fister noted, almost gleefully. "We all die at some point."

"Your date with the grim reaper will be determined by your value and the information you share. If you want to continue breathing, you need to help us get Reese and Alison back safely. If you don't, I wouldn't be surprised if old Winston himself did the honors of ending your life. I understand he was a pretty good marksman during the first world war."

Fister grinned. "Having Winston take me out personally. Not a bad way to go." He said it as if the thought brought him some kind of sick joy.

Fister sighed. "Clay, you bore me. Everything's black and

white to you. You think this is all about good and evil. If I'm not on FDR's side, I must be on Hitler's payroll."

"You have just defined the times we live in."

"What if I'm on neither?"

"No one can be neutral. You're either on the right side or the wrong side."

Fister smiled. "You're wrong, Clay. War offers tremendous opportunities for profit. Poor men die so wealthy men can become even wealthier."

"What are you saying?"

"There are profiteers in your midst. You work with them. You think they're all draped in the American flag. But the people I'm talking about are draped in green dollars rather than red, white, and blue patriotism. They'd sell their souls and their country for what you Americans call bucks. But they're not Nazis."

What was Fister talking about? Was he just killing time? Or hinting at something profound?

Either way, the cocky prisoner had just revealed his Achilles' heel.

Barnes pushed back his chair and exited the small room without another word to Fister. If he was right, he had to track down Helen Meeker. And fast.

CHAPTER 5

Tuesday, March 17, 1942
4:07 PM
St. Louis, Missouri

Helen Meeker drove her yellow Packard to New York, where she caught a military plane to St. Louis. At just past four in the afternoon in the "Show Me" state, she booked a commercial flight to Little Rock. While waiting in the airport for the plane to arrive, she used a pay phone to call her office at the White House, grateful that phone service was back up.

"Good to hear from you, Miss Meeker," said Rose, the receptionist on duty at this hour. "The president told me to expect your call."

"Any messages for me?"

"Just one. Clay Barnes. He's in Albany."

Meeker grabbed a pen and paper from her purse. "Did he leave a number?"

"Jupiter 2-7500."

"Got it. I need to call him right away. Please tell the president I'll check in when I have news."

"Will do."

Meeker pushed the lever down on the pay phone, then let it back up. When she heard a dial tone, she pressed the O key. When the Bell Telephone operator came on the line, Meeker provided her identification, call authorization code, and the number in Albany. Three operators and four minutes later, the Secret Service agent answered.

"Is that you, Helen?"

"Yeah." Considering the recent storms, the connection was surprisingly good. "You have some updates for me?"

"I called the college. Your sister isn't there, but the school doesn't consider her to be missing. She's on a geology field trip at a state park. She's with four other students and a professor. They checked into a lodge yesterday. So apparently Fister was bluffing."

"Did you speak to Alison?"

"No. But the official at the college told me they're probably out on trails, looking at rock formations. Most likely won't come in till after dark."

"Until I hear her voice, I won't be convinced. Where is this park?"

"About an hour and a half northwest of Little Rock. It called Petit Jean."

"I'm at the St. Louis airport right now, waiting for a flight to Little Rock. Can you have a car ready for me at the airport so I can drive up there tonight?"

"I'm a step ahead of you. There's a vehicle the FBI grabbed in a recent raid just waiting for you. It's not a new model, but they claim it runs good."

As long as it got her to the park, she'd be happy. "What's the name of the professor in charge of this outing?"

"Dr. William Manning."

After jotting down the name, Meeker asked, "You get anything from Fister?"

"He talks a lot, but not about anything that matters. The FBI has him now, but I doubt they'll get much either. To him this is all a game."

"Spying is hardly a game."

"Oh, he refuses to admit he's working for either the Germans or the Italians. He talked about some organization he's a part of, but he didn't name it. Just kept rambling about money and power and how we're all blind as to who is really running the show."

"He can lie with the best of them." Meeker knew that from personal experience. "Did the FBI find anything at The Lord's Rest?"

"They dug four bodies out of the rubble. But the lab can't identify who they are. Until they identify one of them as Reese, I'm going to assume he's alive."

"I hope you're right. You got any other leads?"

"Well …" Barnes paused. "There is something unique about this whole mess."

"What's that?"

"The FBI checked into the medical workup Fister had when he was examined at Walter Reed a couple of weeks ago. All the chest wounds checked out just as he said they happened in Germany."

"That's not a shock. I would expect his cover to match in every detail."

"More surprising is Fister's blood type. He's B negative. Very rare."

Meeker shrugged. "That's what I am."

"Well, the two of you are in less than two percent of the world population. But it gets stranger."

"Go on."

"Fister's blood is unlike anything the doctors have ever seen. It seems almost supercharged to enhance healing. The place where you shot him looks like it's a few weeks old, not hours."

A chill raced down Meeker's spine. "That is odd." She wondered if the Nazis were on the verge of creating some kind of new super-warrior.

"The FBI doctors have taken blood samples. Rebecca Bobbs is studying them in the lab now."

"I suggest you alert the president to that news."

"Will do."

A series of load speakers droned, "Flight seventy-seven to Little Rock is now boarding."

"I've got to go. But first, tell me who's meeting me in Little Rock."

"An FBI agent named George Wheeler. He knows the area and the people. Used to work as a state patrolman. I informed him that you will be driving to the park."

"Good." Meeker smiled. "Call him if you get any new information while I'm on my flight."

"You got it."

Meeker dropped the phone into the cradle, grabbed her bag, and rushed to the gate. After presenting her ticket, she climbed the portable steps into the DC-3's cabin, found a seat, and all but fell into it. She needed sleep, but it didn't come easily. After thirty minutes of tossing and turning, she finally dropped off into a fitful slumber, where she was haunted by the image of Reggie Fister's sly grin.

CHAPTER 6

Tuesday March 17, 1942

5:10 PM

Ten miles south of Springfield, Illinois

Fredrick Bauer strode down the steps into the barn's underground chamber. At the bottom of the stairs he stopped, the air causing his nose to burn. The lab reeked of a bizarre combination of ether and gunpowder. The strange mishmash of odors made him smile. The work he'd ordered was being done.

Emma sat behind her desk, dressed in her usual straight black skirt, simple white blouse, and flats. She didn't look up from the file she was reading until he reached her desk.

"Snider is operating now," she reported.

"Good." Bauer glanced toward the surgical area, which was surrounded by a series of pulled curtains. The plan was on schedule. That was all that mattered.

"He brought a man and a woman with him. I was not introduced to them."

"You don't need to know who they are." Bauer glared at her.

Emma cringed, but she did not argue. "The man set up the shooting, and the woman assisted the doctor, but neither of them said a word the whole time. I found it unnerving." She paused, as if hoping for an explanation, which he did not provide. "So many people who come here never say anything. They just look at me with mournful stares."

"Those people are paid well to do a specific job, and they do it," he snapped. "The world would be a far more efficient place if everyone took their work as seriously as those who visit this facility."

"They could at least exchange a greeting," she muttered. Catching herself, she lowered her gaze. "I'm sorry. I shouldn't have said anything."

"Emma, there are times when too much knowledge is a dangerous thing. By not telling you more than you need to know, I'm actually doing you a favor."

"Yes, sir. I appreciate that. But …"

"But you still want to know why so many of our visitors say nothing when they're here."

She nodded.

Bauer sighed. "They don't speak because they can't."

Her face contorted into a look of utter confusion.

"If they could speak, I wouldn't be able to use them."

Emma gazed toward the curtains as if thinking over what she'd just heard. After more than a minute of quiet contemplation, her expression still indicated that she didn't fully comprehend.

"They are mute, Emma."

Her eyes remained locked on the curtain. "All of them?"

Before Bauer could answer, one of the curtains was pulled back. A short, hunch-shouldered, balding man in his sixties emerged, wearing a white surgical gown and cap. He stopped by a trash can, removed the gloves from his long, thin fingers, and lumbered over to the desk. "Would you like a report?"

Bauer touched Emma's shoulder. "Please go to your quarters for about fifteen minutes."

She nodded and climbed the stairs. When he could no longer hear her footsteps on the barn floor, Bauer turn his attention back to the doctor. "You may talk freely now."

Snider sat on the edge of the desk. "Everything is as it should be. Parker and Sullins did their jobs perfectly."

"When can we move him?"

"Within a few hours."

"Good. We should have a location targeted by tonight."

Snider glanced back toward the operating room. "I've heard a rumor," he whispered.

"Rumors are for bored housewives," Bauer snapped. "You are neither bored nor a housewife." Seeing Snider's hurt reaction, he softened his expression and tone. "How long have we known each other, Eric?"

"Twenty years."

"Then don't beat around the bush. Ask me what you want to know."

With a sigh of relief, the doctor leaned close. "I heard we lost the facility in New York."

"It burned down," Bauer said without emotion.

"And the men there?"

"They died."

"I see."

Bauer patted the man's shoulder. "Those we lost were expendable. Better that they died than to fall into the hands of the FBI."

"But I knew one of those men."

"I hired all four of them. But they performed a service, like soldiers on a battlefield. You need to keep your eye on the big picture."

Snider shook his head. "The older I get, the harder that is to do."

Bauer patted his friend's back. "Go back to your mansion in Chicago and relax. Spend some time with your friends at the club. I'll take care of the issues."

Snider wrung his hands. "But what if someone talks? It would ruin me."

"Who knows about your work on this project?"

"The two people who assisted me today."

"And they can't speak. We brought them here blindfolded, so they don't know where this place is. And they don't know your name."

"What about the woman?" Snider shot a glance at the stairway.

"Emma is just another piece of machinery. If she gets too curious or looks like she might reveal us, she will be replaced. And she will never tell her story, I can assure you of that. You have nothing to fear, Eric. So just sit back and enjoy the spoils of your work."

"I guess you're right."

"Of course I am. Now, get out of here. In an hour, two of my associates will arrive to deliver your patient to our handlers in the east. And it would complicate their lives and yours if you were still here when they arrived. You see, they can talk."

Snider stripped off his surgical coat, dropped it on the desk, picked up his jacket, and raced up the steps.

After the doctor was gone, Bauer turned his gaze back to the curtains. He smiled. It was almost time.

CHAPTER 7

Tuesday, March 17, 1942
6:33 PM
Little Rock, Arkansas

As soon as Helen Meeker walked out of her plane and into the small airport lobby, she spotted a tall, wide-shouldered man with a broad chin and dark hair. With his black suit, white shirt, and studious glare, George Wheeler looked like Dick Tracy come to life.

When he spotted her, his grimace turned into a grin. "You must be Helen Meeker," he said in a deep voice as he stepped forward and extended his hand.

"And why do I *have* to be Helen Meeker?" she cracked.

"Because Barnes told me you'd be the most beautiful woman on the plane."

She rolled her eyes. After only a few hours of sleep over the last three days, she doubted she looked anywhere close to her best. But she accepted the compliment, and his hand, with a smile.

"You hungry?"

"I had something on the plane."

"Then I'm guessing you want to head for that park. Let me take your bag."

Meeker pulled on her coat over her dark-blue suit as they headed for the exit. Emerging into the cool evening air, she glanced up at the clouds. They looked ominous. "Where's our car?"

Wheeler pointed to the third vehicle along the curb. "It's the black Auburn sedan with the red trim and wheels. Sorry it's such an old model, but my assigned car was in an accident yesterday, so I had to take what I could get."

"Accident?" She raised her eyebrows as he moved toward the driver's side of the Indiana-built car.

He shrugged but didn't bother explaining until they were out of the airport parking lot. "I was tracking a couple of robbery suspects. They held up a bank in Hot Springs and used a stolen Texas car for the getaway. I got them almost to the state patrol roadblock when they opened fire on me. Pretty much destroyed my Ford's lights, radiator, and front tires."

"Did they get away?"

"'Fraid so."

"At least you weren't hurt."

"Not a scratch." He shook his head as if he were disappointed not to have been injured.

She glanced into the wide, deeply padded backseat. "What's

the story on this car?"

"It was used by some hoods that were running a backroom casino in Hot Springs. They were doing pretty well until they tried to muscle in on some of Lucky Luciano's friends."

"Luciano has been in prison for years."

"He still runs things from behind bars."

That didn't surprise her. "His lawyer came to the White House a while back, offering Luciano's service to the war effort. He claims he has the connections in Europe to get several crime families involved in the war against the Axis powers."

"He probably does have some pull. He's got his fingers in all kinds of things in Hot Springs. And his New York operation may not be as strong as it once was, but it's still bringing in the cash."

Whoever said crime doesn't pay clearly didn't know what he was talking about.

Wheeler downshifted and made a right turn. "The men who owned this car made the wrong guys mad, and they ended up at the bottom of the Ouachita River. The FBI gathered up the spoils, including this beauty. It might not look modern, but I like the art-deco styling, and it handles nicely. Takes the curves as well as any car I've ever driven."

"Pull over," Meeker ordered.

"Why?"

She grinned. "I want to see what this thing will do."

He parked on the side of the road. "Barnes warned me about you."

"Then get ready to hang on," she suggested.

After they switched seats, Wheeler asked, "Hey, aren't you

supposed to be catching me up on why you're here?"

"Don't worry. I can do that and drive at the same time."

CHAPTER 8

Tuesday, March 17, 1942

7:00 PM

Petit Jean State Park, Arkansas

The trip to the lodge should have taken about two hours, but with Helen Meeker driving, she and George Wheeler arrived in just under ninety-five minutes. They left a lot of Goodyear rubber on the Arkansas curves, and the FBI agent seemed to have aged at least five years.

Meeker was at the check-in counter by the time the woozy agent had pulled himself together and entered the rambling, one-story, rock-and-log building. She ignored Wheeler's ashen face and focused on the short, thin, gray-headed park ranger. "My name is Helen Meeker. I'm with FDR's office. My associate is with the Little Rock branch of the FBI. His name is George Wheeler."

"I'm John Stacks. Do you need rooms?"

"No, we need information. Some students from Ouachita College are here on a field trip. The man in charge is a professor named Manning."

"Dr. Bill." Stacks grinned. "We love that guy. He brings students up here all the time."

"Are he and his group here now?"

"Haven't seen them since supper last night." The ranger rubbed his jaw. "But their car is here, so they must be in the park. Is something wrong?"

"I hope not. Could you take us to their rooms?"

"Sure." Stacks grabbed a set of brass-plated keys and stepped out from behind the counter. "Follow me."

Meeker and Wheeler followed their guide out the front door of the main lodge, across a native-stone patio, to the lodge's far wing. When they got halfway down the hall, he stopped at room 11 and knocked. No one answered. He repeated his efforts at 13 and 15, with the same results.

"Guess they're out." He shrugged. "You want me to open one?"

Meeker nodded.

Stacks unlocked the door to a small, cedar-walled, simply furnished room with a bed, dresser, small desk, and two chairs. "Dr. Bill must still have them out on the trail."

"They aren't out there," Meeker said.

"How do you know?"

She pointed to the far side of the room. "Those shoes are covered with mud. So are the clothes on the dresser. Clearly the girls came back from the hike, cleaned up, and changed clothes."

"What about the guys?" Wheeler asked.

They checked the other two rooms and found work clothes and muddy boots there as well.

"They're not in the dining room," the ranger noted. "I would've seen them walk by the front desk." He looked at the clouds. "With rain threatening, I doubt they'd be outside. Not in their good clothes."

"Where is their car?" Meeker asked.

"It's in the same parking space it's been in since they arrived two days ago. You want to see it?"

She shook her head. "If it hasn't moved, that would be a waste of time." Meeker ran her fingers through her dark auburn hair, took a final look around the room, and stepped back into the hall. With the men following, she exited the building and marched back to the main lodge.

She glanced into the dining room. A half dozen people, all over forty, sat in the large open area, enjoying a game of cards. A pot-bellied, balding man with twinkling eyes and a broad smile sported a six-sided silver star on his chest.

Meeker was about to cross the room to talk with this local sheriff when the phone on the counter rang.

Stacks picked it up. "Hello?" After a short pause, he said, "Yes, he's here. Just a second." The ranger walked to the dining room entrance and yelled out, "Paul, it's for you."

The lawman nodded to his friends, dropped his cards on the table, and lumbered to the desk. After silently acknowledging Meeker and Wheeler, he took the phone from Stacks. "This is Sheriff Faulkner. What do you need?" After a few moments, he said, "I'll be there in half an hour to pick him up. Keep your eye on him and try to keep him calm."

As he set the receiver back into the cradle, the ranger asked, "Something wrong?"

"Not really." Faulkner shook his head. "Old Jed is at the sauce again. Seems he barged into Mable Landis's house acting like he'd seen a ghost. She got him settled down, but I need to get over there and take him to the jail to sleep it off."

"Excuse me, Sheriff," Meeker said, taking a step toward the large man. "Could I ask you a few questions?"

Faulkner raised his eyebrows and smiled. "Been a long time since a pretty young thing like you asked me for anything. What can I do for you, ma'am?"

"My name is Helen Meeker. I work for the president. This is George Wheeler. He's with the FBI. We're looking for a group of students from Ouachita College. We have reason to believe foul play might be involved."

"Oh, I doubt that." The lawman shot her a smile that was probably meant to be comforting. "Kids get lost on hikes all the time when they want to, uh … have a good time. What with the war going on, a lot of them are trying to get their good times in now, because they don't know how many they'll have. I'm sure your group will turn up eventually."

"I'm not so sure." Meeker bristled at the man's insinuation and lack of concern. "One of those kids is my sister, and there are some people who might be trying to use her to settle a score with the president."

"I see." Faulkner's easygoing demeanor turned serious. "I

haven't seen anything suspicious. But if you want to follow me to Morrilton, I'll be happy to do what I can—once I get Jed squared away."

"Thanks." She turned to Sparks. "Don't let anyone into those rooms. They need to stay locked until we have a chance to fully investigate them."

CHAPTER 9

Tuesday, March 17, 1942

7:35 PM

Ten miles south of Springfield, Illinois

Fredrick Bauer watched the two big men push his prisoner into a 1938 Oldsmobile sedan. They weren't as gentle about it as Bauer would have liked, but as long as they got the human parcel to its destination alive, it didn't matter.

"When do you need him in New York?" the taller one asked.

"Things are moving faster than I figured they would," Bauer replied. "They're transporting our man tomorrow night. So I need this cargo to be outside of Albany by five in the afternoon. You got that, Mr. James?" Bauer sneered, using the man's pseudonym.

"Yes, sir."

"The address of the safe house is in the packet I gave you when you and Franks arrived. So is half the cash. I'm sure I don't have to remind you of the price you'll pay if you fail me."

The broad-shouldered, dark-headed man stood straighter. "You've made that clear every time we've worked together. But we haven't missed yet."

"Clearly not, or you wouldn't be standing here," Bauer stated. "Now, listen closely. There will be two men in the safe house. You'll call them Smith and Jones. They will respond by saying, 'You must be James and Franks.' If you don't hear those names, they're not the right men. Got it?"

The man nodded.

"After the introductions, you will say a sentence that includes the words 'Boston Red Sox.' They will respond by saying something about Babe Ruth. You will answer with a phrase that includes 'Worst trade ever.' If you mess up on any of that, they will kill you—no questions asked. If they mess up, you kill them, and then call me for further instructions."

"That's a lot of checks and balances."

"There have to be. The FBI and the Secret Service are in on this now. We need to make sure they haven't captured Smith and Jones and substituted someone else for them."

The man grinned, his open mouth showing a gap between his front teeth. "Are their real names actually Smith and Jones?"

Bauer raised a brow. "Are you two really James and Franks?" He stuck his hands in his pockets and shook his head. "Look, I don't care what their real names are, and I don't want to know. It's safer for everyone that way. But I know where to find them if I need to get rid of them."

War was a cold business. It had to be conducted without

emotion and with little regard for human life. Loyalties couldn't shift. And though Bauer realized that James and Franks knew that, he still felt a need to emphasize that they were always one mistake away from the grave.

He turned his attention to the two men standing beside the massive automobile. "If all of the passwords are delivered perfectly, you turn your package over to them."

James shrugged. "Wish all the jobs you gave us were this simple."

Bauer gave him a cold stare. "Getting the package to the destination in less than twenty-four hours won't be easy."

James chuckled. "We have a plane waiting on the outskirts of Springfield. We'll make it with time to spare."

"Is the pilot someone you trust?"

"Without question." Franks stood tall. "I'm the pilot, and it's my plane. And as far as the Feds are concerned, I'm delivering materials to an industrial plant in New York. And since I picked up a shipment of radio tubes in St. Louis this morning that has to be in New York tomorrow, our cover is perfect."

Bauer narrowed his eyes at Franks. "Just make sure no one sees our package."

"They won't. I have a hidden baggage area just for special items like this."

Bauer yanked his hands out of the pockets of his overcoat and ambled to the car. He glanced through the back window at the bound and gagged man lying on the floorboard. He wasn't ready to write Reggie Fister off yet. It was time to play his trump card.

CHAPTER 10

Tuesday, March 17, 1942
11:44 PM
Morrilton, Arkansas

"They're back, I tell you. They want their money, and I don't have it!"

Helen Meeker stared at the disheveled little man sitting in an old wooden chair in front of the sheriff's desk. If ever someone fit the term *loony*, this poor guy was it. The sad human being had slipped into a world where nightmares were real and daily life was a fantasy.

"Two of them held a gun on me today. They're really serious now. You have to believe me!"

Jed Tanner, dressed in worn-out brown dress pants, a tattered and dirty white shirt, scuffed black shoes, and a shiny tan suit jacket, could not sit still. He was dripping with sweat in spite of the chill in the air. His wild green eyes constantly dashed from one side of the room to the other. His thinning blond hair looked as though it hadn't been combed in weeks, and he was three days beyond needing a shave.

The last time Meeker had seen someone like this was in a psych ward. And that was where this poor man needed to be.

After crossing and recrossing one leg over another, and slapping at some unseen creature that he seemed to believe was hovering in the air just above his head, Tanner continued his rant. "I wanted to give them their money. I really did. But we ran out." His eyes found Faulkner. "They trusted me, Paul, and I failed them. And they won't let me forget it. They'll never leave me alone!"

The heavyset sheriff crossed the room and switched on a 1937 console-model Aircastle radio. After it warmed up, he moved the dial until he found a station playing big-band music. As the strains of Kay Kyser's version of "The White Cliffs of Dover" played, the wild man in the chair began to calm down. Within seconds he was relaxed and humming along with the band.

With the situation now under control, Faulkner signaled for Meeker and Wheeler to follow him outside. Once the door was closed, the sheriff pulled a pack of Camels from his pocket and tapped one out into his hand. "Want one?"

Meeker shook her head. Wheeler said, "I don't smoke."

After putting the cigarette between his lips, Faulkner pulled out a lighter, flipped the top, and lit the rolled tobacco. After a few puffs he looked at the nearly vacant downtown street. "Jed was the president and owner of State Bank when the Depression hit." His voice had the cadence and tone of an undertaker. "There was a run on the bank. He kept paying people until there was no cash left. A lot of his customers lost everything they had. Most of them recovered eventually. Jed never did. He spent some time in a mental hospital, but after he was released, his nightmares continued to haunt him. He started drinking almost nonstop. But there isn't enough booze in the world to allow him to forgive himself."

"What kind of nightmares did he have?" Wheeler asked.

"Mostly about a farm family coming into the bank with their three little kids and their elderly grandmother, pleading with him for their money. See, the Bakers left town not long after they came into the bank asking for their money. Since Jed couldn't give them any, they headed to California to hopefully find work. They were all killed in a traffic accident in Oklahoma. When Jed heard about their deaths, he fell apart. Even tried to kill himself, but the doctor got the poison pumped out in time."

The sheriff glanced in the window. "Music is about all that calms him down these days." He took a few more puffs, then tossed the cigarette butt onto the sidewalk and watched it burn for a few seconds before stepping on it with this boot. "I thought he'd sobered up. I would've sworn he hadn't had a drink in months. But it looks like he fell off the wagon."

Meeker tapped her heel on the sidewalk. While this was a mildly interesting story, the clock was ticking. It was almost midnight and she hadn't found her sister. "Sheriff, we need to find out if anyone in town saw the missing students."

As if he hadn't even heard her, Faulkner's eyes remained locked on a corner a block to the south. "The old bank building's down there. It looks pretty much the same as it did on the day of the run. No one ever bought it. Not surprising. I mean, what can you do with a bank building?"

The sheriff shook his head. "Even though he doesn't own it anymore, Jed still has the keys. He goes in there when he's having one of his spells. Countless times I've found him inside the vault on his hands and knees, trying to find money. So sad. And I think he's actually getting worse."

"How so?" Wheeler asked.

"His hallucinations are becoming stranger and more vivid. Instead of ghosts from the Baker family, now he's claiming to see two men with guns." Faulkner continued to study Tanner. "No one ever held a gun on him in real life. Guess he's just slipping deeper into the fantasy world he calls home."

Meeker strolled over to the window and glanced in at the little man. "You say these episodes are triggered by alcohol?"

Faulkner's sad eyes reflected his deep concern for his friend. "When he's sober, he's still haunted, but not delusional."

"I stood right next to him," Meeker said. "I didn't smell any booze."

Leaving the two men to puzzle over her observation, she opened the office door and returned to Tanner's side. She leaned close to the man's face and took a deep breath. Satisfied he hadn't been drinking, she turned off the radio, ending Woody Herman's "Blues in the Night" before it finished. The puzzled man glanced up at her. "Mr. Tanner," she said softly, "my name is Helen. Did you go to the bank tonight?"

He shook his head. "Not tonight. Earlier today."

"And was the Baker family there?"

"No. Got some new customers this time. I guess they wanted to open an account. I told them we didn't have any money. Tried to direct them to the National Bank. But they never said a word."

"Did they have guns?"

"Two of them did. And one of them tried to shoot me. But when he pulled the trigger, the gun didn't fire."

"What happened then?"

"They shoved me into the safe with the others."

"What others, Jed?"

"There was an older gentleman and four young people. Two girls and two boys,."

"How did you get away?"

After swatting at something only he could see, Tanner closed his eyes.

"Jed, what happened to the other people? Do you know where they went?"

Jerking his shoulders from side to side, the little man rubbed his hand over his face. Then he looked off into the distance. "The two men with guns came into the vault with us. While one of them aimed a gun at us, the other one started beating up the kids. I wanted to make him stop. And then I realized I could. And it was easy too."

Meeker gently touched Tanner's shoulder. "Jed," she whispered, "how did you stop the man from beating on the kids?"

He shook his head. "I thought it was a nightmare. I figured if I couldn't see it, it wouldn't be real."

"What did you do, Jed?"

"When they weren't watching me," he explained with a sly

grin, "I snuck out of the vault and closed the door. But it didn't work. Even after I shut it, they were still in my head." He stood and yelled, "They won't leave me alone!"

"You locked them in the safe?" she shouted over the man's screams.

"Yes."

Meeker looked to the sheriff. "The students and the men who took them are locked in the bank vault. We have to get them out before they run out of air." She returned her attention to Tanner. "Jed, you have to open that vault."

"I can't," he cried. "I don't know the combination. They changed it after the bank failure."

Meeker glanced at the sheriff. "Is that true?"

"Sure is. And the man who had it changed died in 1939. Nobody knows how to open that vault."

"My Lord," Tanner sobbed, his eyes wide. "They were real people. And I killed them." Falling to his knees, he grabbed his head and screamed loud enough to wake the dead.

CHAPTER II

Wednesday, March 18, 1942
12:09 AM
Morrilton, Arkansas

After climbing the five twenty-foot-wide concrete steps of the State Bank building, Helen Meeker used Jed Tanner's key to open the deserted bank's ten-foot-tall, windowed door. As she entered the dark, cold building, her heels echoed on the marble floor. While not frantic, she was deeply concerned. If she was going to save the people Tanner had locked in the vault, she'd have to move quickly. Based on what the deranged man had said, they'd been in there at least six hours.

The sheriff and the FBI agent followed her inside.

"I don't suppose there's any power in here," she muttered.

Faulkner ran his hand up the plaster wall to the right of the door and pushed a button. Three blubs dimly lit the interior of the fifty-year-old brick building.

With its thirty-foot ceiling, brass light fixtures, and etched walls, this must have been one of the most impressive small-town banks in Arkansas at one time. Now it was a ghost of what had been … and perhaps a tomb to what could be.

"The city pays the electric bill," the sheriff explained as Meeker and Wheeler looked around the lobby. "It's safer to have power than not to. Besides, we're still trying to find a buyer for this place."

"Where's the vault?" Meeker asked.

"Through the main room and to your right."

She marched past six teller cages and a large table sporting pens, deposit slips, and complimentary calendars for 1929. Toward the back of the lobby were two offices. Tanner's name was painted on the frosted glass of the room to her right. Just beyond that office was a fifteen-by-fifteen-foot metal door with what looked like a large ship's wheel in the center of it.

"That vault is bigger than my office on the inside," Faulkner said. "When I was a kid, I thought it could hold all the money in the world."

"That's good," Wheeler noted. "The larger the area, the greater supply of air for the people inside."

Meeker grabbed the large metal wheel and pulled. The door didn't move. She made a fist and banged it against the door.

"They can't hear you," the sheriff said. "The door and walls are almost two feet thick."

She stared at the round lock in the center of the wheel. "And no one knows the combination?"

"Not anyone who's still alive," Faulkner said. "And there's

not a locksmith in the state who could open this thing. Drills would wear out before doing any real damage."

Wheeler stepped into the office beside the vault and studied the adjoining wall. "Is the chamber as deep as this room?"

"They're exactly the same depth," Faulkner said.

After strolling back to the lobby, the agent pulled a pencil from his pocket and grabbed a deposit slip from the table. He jotted something down, studied his notations, then announced, "Based on my calculations, they can likely stay alive for another seven to ten hours."

"How do you know that?" the sheriff asked.

Wheeler shrugged. "I actually had a question about people locked in an airtight room in one of my college algebra classes. I was the only one to get it right."

Meeker turned to the sheriff. "Maybe the people who made this safe could tell us how to open it."

Faulkner sighed. "The manufacturer was in San Francisco. But they're out of business now."

She raked a hand through her hair, trying to stay focused. She couldn't lose her head just because her sister was likely inside. She had to treat this as objectively as any other problem or she'd go crazy.

"I can't imagine what they must be going through in there," Wheeler mumbled. "Locked in a soundproof room, with no idea whether anyone even knows they're there. The situation must seem hopeless."

Ignoring the ominous thought, Meeker studied the vault door's smooth, cold metal. "When you can't do something yourself," she whispered to herself, "you go to an expert." She looked back at the sheriff. "Is your office unlocked?"

He nodded.

"Good. You two stay here and try to come up with a viable idea. I'm going to go make a phone call."

Meeker rushed out of the bank, barreled down the steps, and ran the block to the sheriff's office as fast as she could in high heels. Not bothering to close the front door, she raced across the room and sank into the seat behind the desk. Panting, she lifted the receiver and dialed zero. When the operator came on she asked for Long Distance. Ten minutes later FBI agent Collins answered.

"Do you know what time it is?" he moaned after she identified herself.

Meeker was all too keenly aware of the passing of time right now. "I need to talk to Stan, the lock expert from the robbery we foiled at the Continental Bank on March fifth."

"But he's in the city jail right now—thanks to you."

"I know. But there are some people trapped in a locked bank vault, and I need a pro to get them out."

"Is it on a time lock?"

"No. The bank closed up shop more than a decade ago, and the man who knew the combination is dead. I've got to get this thing open or seven people will die."

"Even if Stan Weiss could handle the job, he couldn't get there in time."

"I realize that," Meeker snapped, "but he might know someone in this area who could. I'm at the sheriff's office in

Morrilton, Arkansas. The number is Madison 4-6551. Have Stan call me here as soon as possible."

"Will do," Collins replied.

"And just in case Stan doesn't know anyone good in Arkansas or Oklahoma, call the office and get them digging through the files to find a safecracker."

"I'll call them on my way to the jail." Collins hung up.

CHAPTER 12

Wednesday, March 18, 1942
1:29 AM
Morrilton, Arkansas

As she sat in the sheriff's swivel chair, impatiently waiting for the call from Collins about a safecracker, Helen Meeker considered her limited options. Beyond what she had just put into motion, she could think of none.

As the Seth Thomas wall clock ticked minutes away, she tried to remain calm and focused. But with lives hanging in the balance, time seemed to be racing by.

At half past one, the phone finally rang. She snatched up the receiver and jammed it to her ear. "Helen Meeker."

"Long-distance call from the Washington DC city jail."

"Put it through."

"Miss Meeker, this is Stan Weiss. Agent Collins told me what's going on. He said if I help you I can get a break in my sentence. Is that true?"

"I work for the president, Stan. I can make it happen."

"What do you need?"

Meeker brought the man up to speed. "No one knows the combination to the vault. And the company that made it is out of business."

"Was the company located in San Francisco?" Weiss asked.

"How did you know?"

"Safetylock is the only major safe maker that's no longer in the game. They went under in 1933. Their machines are hard to crack. Guys like me hate them."

"Not what I wanted to hear," Meeker muttered.

"That doesn't mean I can't do it. But it would take me a good hour or so. Most safes I can open in less than ten minutes. But even if I got on a plane right now, I couldn't get to where you are in time to save those people."

"I realize that. Is there anyone in this area who could do the job?"

"Only one that I know of. Casper Light. Folks call him Fingers. He's serving a twenty-year stretch in Malvern, Arkansas. He's got a lot of talent, but he's as mean as a snake. Don't ever turn your back on him. I did that once."

Meeker searched through the sheriff's desk drawers for a map. Finding one, she unfolded it. After thirty seconds she spotted Malvern. Doing some quick math, she figured Fingers could get to her location in about three hours.

"Thanks, Stan. I'll see you get a break."

"I appreciate that. At my age, there's no telling how much longer I'll last in stir."

"Is Agent Collins with you?" she asked.

"Yeah."

"Put him on, please."

A few seconds later the FBI agent was on the line.

"Collins, I need you to get the prison to transport Casper Light here to do the job."

"I'll do what I can."

"You can't drag your feet on this. Seven people will die if we don't get them out by six o'clock."

"Got it."

"Call me at this number in one hour. In the meantime, I'll go back to the bank and fill in Wheeler and Faulkner on what's going on."

"Good luck."

"Thanks. We'll need it."

Meeker figured it would take Collins at least a half hour to spring Fingers from the Malvern unit of the Arkansas Penal System. But that was only the beginning of the process. Would the state troopers be able to bring the safecracker to Morrilton, and would the convict be able to free the seven vault prisoners from a sure date with death?

Never had the clocked ticked so loudly or the minutes moved so quickly.

CHAPTER 13

Wednesday, March 18, 1942
5:55 AM
Morrilton, Arkansas

"What time is it?" Helen Meeker asked George Wheeler as she paced in front of the vault.

The agent, who was sitting in an old chair near the bank's front door, checked his watch. "A few minutes before six."

She inhaled a quick breath. "How much time do we have to open the vault before it runs out of air?"

He shrugged. "Somewhere between one and four hours."

That was far too big a gap. Meeker preferred clear facts over vague estimates.

At the sound of a car outside, the agent glanced out the large plate-glass window that overlooked the streets of the town. "Sheriff's back. Has someone with him."

Meeker held her position. It was too soon for the safecracker to arrive, and right now the only person she wanted to see was

Fingers.

Faulkner strolled into the building accompanied by a black man in a denim jacket, white shirt, bib overalls, and a St. Louis Browns baseball cap. "Helen, George, this is Alf Greene. He runs the garage about a half block behind this building."

"Nice to meet you." Wheeler extended his hand.

"Alf, tell these two folks what you saw yesterday."

The short, thin man crossed his arms over his chest. "About three o'clock, a man walked into my place and handed me a note. It said that he and some friends were having car trouble and he'd pay me a hundred bucks, plus the cost of the parts, to get their vehicle running. So we hopped into my tow truck and drove out to a spot on Highway 154 near Perry, where an old Hudson was pulled over to the side of the road. Two girls, two boys, an older man, and a young, tough-looking guy stood in the woods nearby. As I got out of my truck, I waved, but none of them waved back."

Meeker narrowed her eyes. "You didn't talk to any of them?"

"Nope. And they didn't talk to me."

"Go on," Faulkner said. "Tell the story just like you told it to me."

"When I looked under the hood, I realized the water pump had seized up. Then the belt broke and flew into the radiator, which caused a leak. I told the man with the note that I'd need to get the car back to my shop. Then I'd see if Western Auto had the pump and belt. The guy didn't say anything, but he nodded. I took that as a yes."

Greene ran his hand over his slick head. "After I got the car hooked up to my truck, the guy handed me another note. It said they wanted me to tow the car with all the passengers riding in it. I told him it'd be better for my truck if the Hudson was empty, but the guy shook his head and pulled out a fifty-dollar bill. So I did it their way."

How odd that someone would communicate everything through written notes. Perhaps the man was mute. But were all of his friends unable to speak as well?

"When we got to my garage, the man helped me push the car into my building. The rest of the group walked down the alley. I figured they were going to get something to eat."

Meeker doubted that. More likely they needed a place to hide out for a couple of hours. Probably picked the first vacant building they could get into.

"The man waited at my shop while I went and got the parts. After I came back, he gave me a note asking how long the repair would take. I told him the car would be ready by six, and he walked out my back door. That was the last I saw of him. The car is still in my shop."

"Why do you suppose they didn't speak?" the sheriff asked.

"Maybe they were foreigners," Wheeler suggested.

"But the notes were written in English," Meeker said.

"You need anything else from me?" Greene asked.

"No," Meeker replied. "But thanks for the information."

"You're welcome," the mechanic said with a smile.

Moments after Greene left, another car pulled up to the curb just outside the bank building. Three men got out of the backseat. Two were state patrolmen. The other was a short, thin

ACE COLLINS

man in prison stripes. He was pale, skinny, about six feet tall. His gaunt face was pockmarked, his eyes dark and menacing, and his hands cuffed.

As soon as the three men came through the front door, Meeker led them to the back of the bank. When they reached the vault door, she said, "Get the cuffs off him and let him go to work."

Fingers smiled as one of the lawmen unlocked his hands. After rubbing his bony wrists, he examined the vault door. "Been a while since I've seen one of these. June of 1926, to be exact. In San Diego. We got away with fifty grand on that job."

Meeker ignored his bragging. "Think you can do it again?"

The convict grinned. "I'm one of only five men in the country who can talk to this baby and get it to listen. Assuming you got a stethoscope."

Wheeler reached into his coat pocket, retrieved the medical instrument, and handed it to the safecracker. Fingers cradled it in his hands. "Rene Laennec sure made my work a lot easier."

"Who?" Wheeler asked.

"The Frenchman who invented the stethoscope." Fingers positioned the small tubes into his ears.

"How long?" Meeker demanded.

He knelt before the vault door and placed his right hand on the dial. "Might be less than a minute. Could take an hour."

"Make it closer to a minute, okay?"

He raised an eyebrow. "I need everyone to be as quiet as a church mouse. Just sit back and watch an artist at work."

Holding the stethoscope's bell to the door, Fingers fixated his attention on his work, seemingly unaware that anyone else was in the room. As the minutes passed, everyone but Wheeler found a wall to lean against. He sat in a chair, crossed one leg over the other, popped his neck, and closed his eyes.

Time dragged. Six ten became six thirty and then six fifty. For Meeker every minute was an eternity. Each moment brought those in the vault closer to death.

As she waited, she thought of the few memories she and Alison had created since they reunited. There should have been many more. Why had she let her work get in the way of bonding with her only living relative?

If, by the time the door opened, everyone inside had died, their deaths would be on her head. This wasn't crazy Jed's doing. She bore the full responsibility.

As Meeker mentally beat herself up, the thin man in stripes continued to play with the locking mechanism on the door, his face never changing expression.

At just before seven o'clock, Fingers rose to his knees and smiled.

"Is it done?" Meeker asked.

"There's just one number left."

"Then do it," Meeker demanded.

"As soon as everyone hands me their guns."

"What?" Faulkner barked.

"I want a get-out-of-jail card for opening up this can."

The sheriff pulled out his Smith & Wesson and aimed it the grinning con. "You get back to work or I'll shoot you."

"Then the seven people in this vault will die."

"How do we know you'll finish the job and let them out?"

ACE COLLINS

Meeker asked.

"All I'm asking for is the chance to get away. Just drop your guns at my feet. While you're rescuing the folks inside, I take off."

"We'll catch you before you get very far," one of the troopers taunted him.

"Probably." Fingers shrugged. "But if I get even an hour or a day or a week of freedom before you do, it'll be worth it."

The lead trooper turned to Wheeler. "It's your call."

The FBI agent reached into his coat, pulled out his service revolver, and slid it across the dusty marble floor to the safecracker. The two troopers and Faulkner followed suit. Smiling, Fingers picked up all but one of the weapons and emptied the chambers. The last gun he stuck in his belt.

"Where are the keys to your car?" Fingers asked the sheriff.

"In the ignition."

"You parked right in front of the one they brought me up here in?"

"Yep."

The safecracker looked to the lead trooper. "And where's your car key?"

"In my pocket."

"Slide it over to me."

The cop did as instructed.

"You got what you wanted, now get on with it," Meeker growled.

Fingers turned back to the vault's massive door. He spun the large wheel, then pulled the lever. A second later he yanked the door open about three inches. "It has been a pleasure serving the FBI."

As Fingers made his escape, gun in hand, Wheeler pulled the vault door wide open. Two young men and two women sat in the center of the large, open area.

"Alison," Meeker whispered.

The beautiful college student smiled as she stood. "It took you long enough."

After hugging her sister, Meeker asked, "Are you okay?"

"I'm fine. But one of the two men who kidnapped us died a couple of hours ago. I think he had a heart attack. And Dr. Manning is kind of sick."

Meeker followed her gaze to a pale older man, his eyes red and his shoulders hunched. Behind him stood a large, solidly built young man with a gun in his hand.

When the remaining kidnapper realized his rescuers were unarmed, he darted past them to the main exit and raced out the door.

As the lawmen retrieved their weapons and ammunition, Meeker ran to the lobby, pulled the gun out of her purse, and hurried to the front door. She stepped outside just as the young man was about to enter a grocery store. She aimed her Colt at his left knee. "Stop or I'll shoot."

He turned and raised his gun. Before he could squeeze the trigger, Meeker fired. He fell face forward onto the street. A second later, the two troopers emerged from the bank, brandishing their weapons. One ran toward the downed man. The other got into the patrol car and sped in the direction Fingers had gone.

Meeker stepped back into the bank.

"The man in the vault is dead," Wheeler announced. "I recognize him. His name's Richard Barton. He worked for Lucky Luciano in Hot Springs." The agent scratched his head. "Moving from organized crime to working for the Nazis seems like a strange career choice."

"I clipped the kidnapper so he couldn't fly. Maybe he can explain what's going on."

Wheeler shook his head. "Not going to happen. Barton has no tongue, so I imagine this guy doesn't either."

"Excuse me?"

"Barton's been cut out," he replied matter-of-factly. "Probably the same with all of them."

Meeker shuddered. That explained the notes. But who would do such a thing?

"Too bad the safecracker got away," Wheeler said.

Faulkner chuckled. "He won't go far. My car was running on fumes. I was going to fill it up this morning. Glad I didn't."

Meeker forced a weak smile as she turned to her sister. "Alison, you're coming home with me."

"What about school?"

"We'll work something out. But until we find Henry Reese, I don't want you to be alone. You understand?"

"Yeah. I'll miss my friends, but I wouldn't want anyone to have to go through something like this."

"What's your next move?" Wheeler asked.

"I'm going back to New York," Meeker explained. "I'm hoping the man the FBI is holding can give me the clue I need to find the best partner I ever had."

CHAPTER 14

Wednesday, March 18, 1942
3:11 PM
Rural New York

At just past three in the afternoon, James and Franks drove up to the two-bedroom, white-frame home just outside the small Hudson River town of Cedar View, New York.

"You wait in the car with the package," James ordered as he slipped out from behind the wheel of the rented 1938 Ford sedan. After glancing over his shoulder toward the all-but-deserted highway, he ambled to the house's front stairs. Even though the cold north wind was biting into his cheeks, he climbed the four steps slowly, unsure as to who might be inside.

Once on the stoop, he rapped on the door. A few seconds later it was opened by a mountain of a man more than six and a half feet tall and likely two hundred fifty pounds. His dark complexion and deep black eyes hinted at Native American origins. Behind him stood a man who was six inches shorter but who looked equally strong and menacing.

"I'm looking for Smith and Jones."

The huge form blocking the door replied in voice deep enough to shake a large building, "You must be either James or Franks."

"I'm James. Franks is in the car with the package." He adjusted his tie, then added, "He's a Boston Red Sox fan."

"I always liked Babe Ruth."

"Franks still thinks sending the Babe to the Yankees was the worst trade ever."

Smith relaxed a bit, but his expression remained guarded. "Bring the package in. We'll take over from here."

James motioned to Franks, who got out, opened the passenger-side back door, and yanked the human cargo off the floorboard. The guy's mouth was gagged, his hands were bound, and he wore a blindfold.

After standing him up, Franks pushed him across the yard, up the stairs, and to the front door. Smith grasped the captive's shirt collar and pulled him into the house. Jones then led the man out of sight.

Smith reached into his pants pocket, pulled out an envelope, and handed it to James. "You can count it if you want, but it's all there."

Their work done, the men returned to the Ford. James didn't know what was going to happen to the prisoner. But with ten thousand dollars to split with Franks, he didn't much care.

CHAPTER 15

Thursday, March 19, 1942

8:09 AM

American Airlines Flight 39

Helen Meeker and her sister limited their conversations to small talk until after their plane lifted off the runway at the Little Rock airport.

"What's this all about?" Alison asked when the noise in the plane made eavesdropping impossible.

"I can't really tell you very much."

Alison nodded. "But what happened at the park when those men took us has something to do with your work with the president, doesn't it?"

"Yes."

"Do you know who they were?"

"Hired hoods from Cleveland. I interrogated the one who lived. He had no idea why they were doing the job. It was all about a paycheck for them."

Alison shook her head as if she found it hard to believe anyone would make a living like that.

"He told me that after the deadline passed he would have set you free, but I didn't believe him. You could identify them. So whoever hired them probably would have ordered them to kill you if things hadn't worked out the way they did."

"Not a very cheery thought." The girl sighed as she let her head fall back against the plane's seat.

Meeker shrugged. "It's a cruel world. Especially these days. Human life is as cheap as it has ever been. People seem to trade life with as little emotion and far less thought than folks on Wall Street trade stocks and bonds."

A stewardess walked up from the back of the plane and leaned over toward Meeker. "Nice to see you again, Helen."

She introduced the woman to Alison.

"The pilot just received a radio message that there will be a military plane in St. Louis for you two. A man will meet you at the airport gate and take you to your flight to New York."

Meeker smiled. "Thank you."

"My pleasure." The young woman straightened. "Love your suit. Where'd did you find it?"

"I didn't pack enough clothes for the trip, so my sister and I did some shopping yesterday. I found this in a store in downtown Little Rock. I think it was called Kathryn's."

"Next time we have a layover there, I'll have to check it out. Would you ladies like anything to drink?"

Meeker looked to Alison, who shook her head. "We're fine."

As the stewardess returned to the back of the plane, Alison leaned close to her sister. "Those men who kidnapped us never said a word, not to us or even to each other. Did you get the one you captured to talk to you?"

"Not exactly. He explained through written notes that they'd agreed to be made mute as a requirement for getting jobs. They each got twenty-five thousand dollars in exchange for having their tongues cut out." A shiver raced up her spine. "They didn't even know where the surgery was performed. They were blindfolded the entire time."

"Who would let someone take their voice away?"

Meeker took a moment to formulate her answer. "It happens all the time. But usually the people who let someone take their voices can still talk. They just stop doing it."

Alison's forehead puckered. "What are you saying?"

"If you don't read, study, and think for yourself, then your words are just a reflection of what other people tell you. That's what happened in Germany. The people lost their voice to Hitler. In fact, they freely gave their voices to him. They allowed him to call the shots and they did nothing but cheer. The ideas they embrace, the words they systematically repeat, are nothing more than directives placed in their minds and spewed out of their mouths, with little connection to their own thoughts. People like that might as well have their tongues cut out, because they've fallen into a cult-like mentality that feeds them slanted views and assures them that those opinions are the only ones that have substance."

Alison stared at her with wide eyes. "I just wanted to know why someone would allow someone else to cut out their tongue."

"I know." Meeker locked eyes with her sister. "But please promise me you'll find out what all sides think about an issue and then make up your mind based on what you believe, not what others tell you to believe. Because that's basically what this war is all about. We're fighting for the right to think and speak about and believe whatever we want. Having a press that gives a voice to all sides of an issue will prevent monsters like Hitler from rising to power."

The startled look on her sister's face made Meeker realize she'd been preaching. "Let's talk about something else. Why don't you tell me about the boys you like at school."

While she tried to focus on Alison's story about a young man named Cliff, her mind drifted to a man whose kiss still lingered on her lips. If Henry Reese died, she would never forgive herself for not telling him how she felt about him.

CHAPTER 16

Thursday, March 19
7:55 PM
Albany, New York

"You still have time to tell me what I need to know," Clay Barnes announced as he walked into the small, stark, brick cell at the Albany Police Station. "After all, your house of cards is falling apart."

Reggie Fister, dressed in prison stripes, grinned at the Secret Service agent. "Oh, I think it's your house that needs repair. Mine is still pretty strong. Especially since I'm holding two powerful wild cards. After all, you Americans are pretty sentimental when it comes to human life. I don't see you allowing Alison Meeker or Henry Reese to die just to keep me in custody."

Barnes looked at his watch. It was almost eight. Though Fister hadn't slept in days, he was nowhere near breaking. Still, since the man was going to be transported to a maximum-security unit soon, he decided to take one more shot at rattling the prisoner.

"You don't hold either of those wild cards anymore, Reggie."

Fister's head jerked and his eyes locked onto Barnes. "You're bluffing."

"Nope." He folded his arms and leaned against the cold brick wall. "Alison was freed earlier this morning and we have one of the two men who snatched her. The other one is dead."

For the first time, Fister actually looked surprised. "He won't talk."

"Obviously not." Barnes laughed. "But from what I hear, he's pretty prolific with a pencil. The FBI agent in Little Rock was even impressed with the guy's spelling."

Fister studied the tabletop for a few moments before returning his gaze to his interrogator. "You said I lost both of my cards."

"Several bodies were found in the rubble of The Lord's Rest. Henry and I were good friends. I hated to lose him. But at least he died doing what he loved."

The prisoner shrugged. "Those cards didn't mean anything anyway. They were merely diversions. And the man you caught can't give you anything you need."

Barnes pushed himself off the wall and strolled toward the door. "We have you, Alison is alive, and Reese died for his country. Game, set, match."

The guard opened the cell door to let Barnes out. Before he left, he added, "Oh, and Nigel Andrews is doing fine. Your shot missed all the vital organs. You can chew on those facts on your trip south."

As he savored his parting shot, a quartet of FBI agents brushed past Barnes. They marched into the cell, snapped handcuffs onto Fister, and led him out the door, down a hall, through a back entry, and to a waiting car. Barnes followed and watched the black Buick depart with someone who had once been considered a hero.

As the car faded from sight, he heard the clicking of high heels behind him. Turning, he looked into the beautiful eyes of Helen Meeker.

"Am I too late to see him off?" she asked.

"Yeah. Reggie Fister is on his way to a place so far removed from freedom that he might never see the sky or feel the warmth of the sun again."

She gazed down the now-vacant alley. "Too bad. I had a couple of questions I wanted to ask him."

"He wouldn't have given you straight answers. I know that from experience. But I did shake him up a little when I informed him that his two trump cards are void."

"We found Henry?" she asked, her voice infused with hope.

"No. But I let Reggie think his body was discovered in the ashes of that old house."

Disappointment clouded Helen's face and made her shoulders sag. "How are they transporting Fister?"

"You'll love this." Barnes chucked. "He's going by freight train, locked in a box car."

Helen chuckled. "Well, I'm heading back to Washington on Highway 9. Maybe I'll wave at the train as I drive by."

He put a hand on her upper arm. "You ought to take a day off. I doubt you've slept much this week."

Helen shook her head. "No days off until after we find Henry."

That didn't surprise Barnes a bit. "How's your sister?" he asked, eager to change the subject.

"She's okay. That girl is a real trooper. She's in the front office right now. I'm planning to keep her close until we get this mess cleared up."

"Good thinking. I'm sure you can find something for her to do at the White House. Can't get much safer than that."

They stood there for a few silent moments, staring down the alley Reggie Fister had just traveled. It was filled to overflowing with trash cans, loose newspapers, and empty bottles. That seemed an appropriate end to the man's saga. He might never tell what he knew. But at least now he could no longer hurt anyone.

CHAPTER 17

Thursday, March 19, 1942
10:18 PM
US Highway 9 West

Helen Meeker's yellow Packard hummed along the highway on a clear night with temperatures in the low forties. Her sister sat in the passenger seat, gazing out the window at the rural countryside. They'd visited enough on the two flights to New York that they no longer needed to talk. Instead they hummed along with the music coming from the car's eight-inch radio speaker.

When familiar strains of a new tune came on the radio, Meeker said, "I know that song. But I don't recognize the singer. Do you know who he is?"

Alison smiled. "You really don't know the dreamy guy who sings 'Night and Day'?"

"Should I?"

"Do you remember the Tommy Dorsey Band's hit 'I'll Never Smile Again'?"

"Of course. I love it."

"Well, this guy was their singer on that record. He sang with Harry James for a while too. But now he's out on his own. The bobby-soxers all think he's dreamy."

"Dreamy?" Meeker laughed.

"Yeah. His name is Frank Sinatra. Frankie is what's buzzin' now."

"Buzzin'?"

"He's been on the radio a lot the past few weeks. He's leading the way and setting the trends."

"If you say so."

Alison giggled. "Really, Helen, you have to catch up on the lingo, get to know the glitterati."

"Glitterati?"

Alison rolled her eyes. "The people who are grabbing the spotlight and making waves. I can't believe you don't know that."

Meeker resisted telling her sister that she'd been too busy saving the free world to keep up with slang terminology. "So, are there other glitterati you like to listen to?" she asked, hoping she'd used the word right.

"Gosh, yes. Freddie Martin, Glen Miller, Sammy Kaye, Benny Goodman. If it swings, I'm with it."

None of the names rang a bell with her. "Sounds like I might have to buy some new records."

"What's that?" Alison pointed to something up ahead.

Seeing a half dozen police cars, Meeker gently applied her brakes. The uniformed officers were stopping each car and searching seats and trunks.

"What do you think they're looking for?"

"I don't know. But hand me my purse. If I've already got my identification out, maybe we can get through this quicker."

As Meeker pulled up behind three other cars, a state trooper approached, holding a flashlight. When he got to her vehicle, she rolled down the window. "Something wrong?"

"A train derailed just ahead. The Feds had a prisoner in one of the cars and he escaped. We're looking for him."

Meeker's heart skipped a beat. She handed the cop her ID. "Was the prisoner's name Fister by any chance?"

"They didn't give us a name, just a description."

"Did the description include a bandage on the man's right hand?"

The trooper's eyes widened. "How did you know?"

"I'm a part of this case." She nodded at her identification.

The man glanced at the papers. "Holy cow, you work for the president."

"Yes. And I know the escaped prisoner, probably better than any of the FBI agents who are running this thing."

He handed the papers back to her. "I'll get on the radio and tell them you're here." He took off at a sprint.

"What's going on?" Alison asked.

Meeker took a deep breath. "The man who escaped from that train is one of the most dangerous people on earth. He's the reason you were kidnapped."

Alison gasped.

The uniformed man returned to the car. "About a mile up the road, there's a two-story, red brick home just off the highway. That's the temporary command center. I told the troopers to let you through."

"Thanks."

Since the cars in front of her had already gone through inspection, Meeker drove up to the roadblock. The officers waved her past the barricade.

Quickly pushing her vehicle up to fifty, she kept her eyes peeled for the meeting point. Seeing a group of men in suits standing at the end of a gravel lane, she turned in. They nodded as she passed.

As she pulled alongside about forty other cars, Meeker saw dozens of men rushing off into the woods and fields in several directions. The chaotic scene looked more like panic than plan.

She shut off the motor and looked at her sister. "I want you to go in with me. But you need to be quiet. Just follow me and try to stay in the background."

"Got it." Alison's tone held excitement. To the college kid, this must seem like the adventure of a lifetime. To Meeker it was a nightmare.

Grabbing her purse, she stepped out of the vehicle. With her sister by her side, she crossed the yard and walked onto the porch. Barnes stood there, waiting for her.

"What happened?"

"The rails were disconnected at a spot in the middle of the woods, just before a bridge. About twenty cars ended up on their sides. The engineer and three firemen are dead."

"And what about Fister?"

"The car with him in it was near the back of the train, so it stayed upright. As soon as one of the FBI agents opened the door, someone tossed in a gas bomb. Before anyone knew what had happened, Fister was gone."

"How can I help?"

"You can identify Fister. So I'd suggest you go with one of the teams and look through houses in the wooded area."

"Sounds good." Meeker glanced at her sister. "What about Alison?"

"She can stay in the house with me."

"You're not joining the search?"

Barnes curled his lips. "The FBI doesn't want Secret Service involved."

Meeker bristled. The ridiculous rivalry between the two agencies caused many irritating delays.

"I'll take care of Alison. You go to the back of the house. Eugene Tyler's team is getting ready to take off."

After a quick hug, Meeker left her sister in Barnes's care.

Someone she knew had set up Fister's escape. Probably someone she talked to on a regular basis. But who?

There was no time to contemplate that right now. She had to help track down Fister before the man made a clean escape.

CHAPTER 18

Thursday, March 19, 1942
11:17 PM
Rural south central New York

Meeker studied FBI Agent Eugene Tyler as they left the command center to begin their search. The small man with a square jaw and dark eyes looked like a human Boston terrier. And his stern appearance fit perfectly with his no-nonsense approach.

He and his team of five men quickly and efficiently went through half a dozen homes and twice as many barns in a little over two hours. Fister was not in any of them.

The seventh home they came to was little more than a shell of a house. The broken windows and missing shingles indicated the building likely hadn't been lived in for at least twenty years.

"If it was a man, it would be a Republican," Meeker quipped.

The agent's brow furrowed. "What did you say?"

She shrugged. "The whole thing is leaning right."

"There is no place for humor in the field," Tyler growled.

Meeker disagreed. Humor was a requirement for sanity in a job like theirs. Clearly this man didn't think so. "Most folks would walk right past this place without a second look. But if you wanted to evade a search party, this would suit you perfectly. Since no one lives here, there's nobody to turn you in."

Tyler turned to his men. "Go in with guns drawn. Search every inch of the place. If there's an old can of beans in the pantry, I want to know about it."

The men hustled to obey their orders.

Tyler looked at Meeker. "You coming in?"

"No. I'll stay here and watch the yard."

He shrugged. "Suit yourself."

It took ten minutes for the men to explore every nook and cranny in the old house. As they reassembled outside the rear of the home, Tyler approached Meeker. "We didn't find anything."

"Not even a can of beans?" Meeker quipped.

Tyler glared at her. "I just hope the other groups are doing better than we are."

The moment the words left his lips, a half-dozen shots rang out from the woods about twenty yards away. Two of the FBI agents fell to the ground, grabbing their shoulders. Everyone scrambled for cover.

After retrieving her Colt from her purse, Meeker crouched behind the south wall of the house, anticipating more fire. There was none.

"Why do you suppose he stopped shooting?" Tyler asked,

kneeling beside her.

"I want to know why he shot in the first place. We weren't onto him. Why would he call attention to himself?"

"Criminals aren't known for being bright," Tyler said, his eyes focused on the place where the gunshots had originated. "Most are impulsive. He probably just panicked."

Meeker shook her head. "I don't know about garden-variety criminals. But I do know Fister. He is anything but impulsive or stupid."

Tyler turned to his men, who were hiding behind nearby trees. "Cover me. On my signal."

Meeker chuckled. "Talk about impulsive and stupid ..."

"I've got a job to do, woman," Tyler barked. "You just stay out of the way."

"It's your party."

Tyler groaned. Then he raised his pistol. "Now, men," he cried out.

The agent, gun blazing, stepped out from behind the house and sprinted toward the woods. The remainder of the team sprayed fire at the point where the shots had originated. Not a single round was returned.

When Tyler made it to the tree line, he stopped and peered into the eerily quiet darkness. He stepped into the woods, then reappeared a few moments later and waved for his party to join him. His team, even the two wounded ones, hurried to join their leader.

Meeker stayed put. "What did you find?" she hollered.

"Nothing," Tyler called back. "Just a few casings."

She shook her head. All those heroics for nothing.

The agents circled around their leader, likely planning their next move. Meeker sat on the ground and pondered the situation. Why would anyone shoot at them? And how had the shooter manage to elude the search party?

An idea hit her. "Tyler," she yelled across the field. "Get over here."

The man marched back to the abandoned house. "You got something?"

"How are the guys who were shot?"

"Lucky. Their wounds are little more than scratches."

"That's what I figured. I don't think the shooter wanted them dead."

Gun ready for action, Meeker crept toward a small, unnatural-looking hill in the otherwise level yard. Using her free hand, she pulled away some brush. "Looks like a root cellar to me."

"Men," Tyler hollered, "get over here." They raced to his side. "Dobbs, open that door. Jenkins, shine your flashlight into the hole. Everyone else, prepare for action."

Meeker put a staying hand on Dobbs's arm. "We need whoever is in there alive. This could be the only person who could reveal whether there was a connection between those shots and the train crash."

Dobbs, a blocky man of average height with coal-black hair and a round face, grabbed the door's handle, swung it open, then quickly backed away. Jenkins's light captured the form of a man huddled just inside the door. He was wearing prison stripes.

"Come out with your hands up," Tyler ordered.

The man staggered forward, hands raised. He stopped ten feet in front of the agents. Though he lacked his usual swagger, Meeker immediately recognized the tall, rugged man with wavy hair and expressive eyes.

"Are you Reggie Fister?" Tyler asked.

"I am," came the soft reply.

CHAPTER 19

Friday, March 20, 1942
2:15 AM
Rural south central New York

Helen Meeker followed FBI agent Eugene Tyler as he escorted his prisoner back to the temporary command center. As they marched Fister into the house, Clay Barnes stepped out onto the porch. "You found him!"

"I did," Meeker acknowledged. "But I'm not sure why."

"What do you mean?"

"It was too easy. Why would someone wreck a train to spring a guy and then hand him right back to us?"

Barnes shrugged. "Maybe they needed something he knew, and after he gave them that information, they had no more use for him."

That made as much sense as anything else. And if it was true, perhaps Fister would roll over on those people now.

She stepped into the home and strode down a hall into the living room, where the captive sat handcuffed to a chair. In the room's bright light, there was no doubt this was Reggie Fister. The man who'd nearly charmed her into bed, and who'd planned on killing the president, now looked like a beaten dog.

"I need to talk to him alone," Meeker said.

"I don't think so," Tyler argued. "We're going to wait until the command leader gets here so he can work the guy over."

"You know, there are still killers on the loose out there. Why don't you and your men go find them?"

Tyler's face turned a deep shade of red. "I've had just about enough of you. I can do my job without the help of a woman. So why don't you just go back to your job as FDR's pet."

Meeker felt her blood boil. "You would never have found Fister if I hadn't discovered his hiding place," she growled. "The least you can do is step aside and let me have a few minutes with him. I've earned that much."

"You've earned nothing," Tyler shot back.

Barnes came into the room "Helen, the president is on the phone. He wants to know what information you've been able to get from Fister. I told him you haven't completed your interrogation yet. He sounded upset."

Meeker hid her satisfied smile and turned to Tyler. "Would you like to take that call and explain to the president of the United States why I haven't finished my job?"

Tyler's shoulders slumped. "I just don't understand why it's so important that you talk to him first."

"Because he might know where Henry Reese is. And since

I know this man better than anyone else, he's more likely to tell me than you." She caught the agent's gaze. "You do want Henry back on the force, don't you?"

"Of course."

"Then give me five minutes with Fister."

"Fine. But you can't talk to him alone."

"Okay. Then let Clay stay in here with me."

Tyler released a long sigh. "Fine. Have it your way."

Barnes smiled. "Let me go tell Mr. Roosevelt what's going on. I'll be right back." The Secret Service agent hurried off.

Meeker and Tyler waited, without making eye contact or conversation, until he returned.

"You've got five minutes," Tyler grumbled. He turned to his men. "Cover the door and windows. Make sure this prisoner does not get away."

After everyone but Barnes had left, Meeker faced Clay. "The president's call came at the perfect time."

Barnes grinned. "There was no call."

Meeker wanted to hug Clay. "Thanks."

She turned her attention to the prisoner. He sat listlessly in the chair, staring blankly ahead, as if unaware of anything going on around him. Seeing him look so disoriented, she almost felt sorry for him. "What is your name?"

"Reginald Fister." His words were slurred and his eyes unfocused.

"You already know who he is," Barnes whispered.

"Yes. But he's obviously been drugged. I asked that question to determine how aware he is."

Meeker lifted Fister's chin and peered into his pale-blue eyes. He didn't react.

Keenly aware of Tyler's five-minute time limit, she noticed blood had soaked through the bandage around Fister's wrist. She ripped off the tape and unwound the gauze. The wound had opened and was slowly dripping blood.

"It looks worse than it did this morning," Barnes observed. "He must have reinjured it trying to escape."

Meeker crouched before the prisoner. "Do you know who I am?"

He shook his head.

Meeker stood. Clearly, she wasn't going to get the information she needed from this shell of a man.

Tyler opened the door and marched in. "Time's up. He's ours now."

"You can have him," Meeker mumbled as she headed for the door.

"Where you going?" Barnes asked.

"Back to Washington." She glanced over her shoulder at Tyler. "When the drugs wear off, let the president know if he says anything."

"Oh, we'll make him talk." The agent's chest puffed with pride.

"We'll see."

CHAPTER 19

Saturday, March 21, 1942
9:07 AM
Washington DC

Helen Meeker was already wide awake when her alarm went off. The president had demanded she get some rest, but her sleep had been fitful, to say the least. She dragged herself out of bed, got dressed, then sat on her bed, staring at nothing in an almost catatonic state.

When she heard a knock on her bedroom door, she croaked out, "Come in."

Alison burst into the room, nearly clapping her hands in excitement. "Are we really going to the White House today?"

"Yes." She took a deep breath and stood.

"I can't wait to meet the president."

"You'll like him." Meeker shuffled to the sink to brush her hair. "He has a dry wit and a quick smile."

"I'm sure he's proud of you for helping to wrap up a huge case."

Alison perched on the edge of the bed and bounced on the mattress. Meeker stared into the mirror at the dark circles under her eyes. After covering them with a bit of makeup, she returned to her room, where her sister stared at her, wide-eyed.

"You caught the man the whole world wanted, but you haven't smiled once since we got home. You look like you've just lost your best friend."

"I may have," she whispered. Each hour that passed meant less of a chance that Henry Reese was still alive.

The ringing phone yanked Meeker out of her morbid thoughts. She picked up the receiver after the second ring. "Helen Meeker."

"This is the overseas operator. You have a call from London. The caller's name is Russell Strickland. Do you want to accept it?"

Meeker racked her exhausted brain, trying to remember where she'd heard that name. Then it came to her. He was the man the preacher was supposed to meet in Mississippi. Reese had told her he was in England now, working with the OSS. She'd asked Henry to track him down and see if he had any leads on Reggie Fister.

"Yes, please. Put him on."

Over a lot of static on the line, and strange noises in the background, she heard, "Miss Meeker?"

"Yes."

"I have a bit of information for you about Reginald Fister."

"Shoot," Helen pleaded as she grabbed a pencil and a scratch pad.

"He was born in a small town in Scotland. His father was Scottish and his mother German. They were both killed in a house fire when Reginald was two years old."

"And my theory about Reggie having an identical twin?" Meeker asked.

A tremendous booming noise sounded over the line. For a moment, she thought the call had been lost. Then Strickland's voice came back. "Sorry about that. The Germans are bombing us today. That last one came rather close."

"Are you safe?"

"I'll get to a shelter after I give you what you need."

"Then hurry, please."

"You were spot on. After the parents died, Alistair Fister was sent to live in a children's home in Germany. Reginald was shipped to the one in Edinburgh. I found no trace of what happened to either of them after that."

"Thanks." Another blast echoed through the phone line. "Now find someplace safe."

"I will."

As soon as Meeker set the receiver back in the cradle, Alison asked, "What was that all about?"

She gazed at her sister. "The FBI has Reggie Fister. But it's not the Fister they need."

"Huh?"

"The real Reggie Fister came to this country as an exchange student," she mused out loud. "But the Nazis nabbed him when they got his twin to spy for them. If the Fister who pretended to be a British hero was ever caught and unmasked, they would replace him with the twin. That was the plan all along. And it was brilliant! The train crash was staged to make the swap. That's why they shot at us … to make sure we found him."

Alison looked confused. "How did they know Fister was on that train?"

"We've got a mole. And I think I might know who it is. But I can't make a move until I'm sure." She grabbed her purse and coat. "You ready to meet my uncle Franklin?"

"More than ready."

"Then get your coat and let's go."

The two women stepped out of the apartment and into a day that felt more like spring than late winter. When they got to Meeker's yellow Packard, Alison slid into the passenger side and immediately flipped on the radio and cranked up the volume. Tommy Dorsey's "Fools Rush In" filled the air.

As Meeker walked past the front bumper of her car, the voice she now recognized as Frank Sinatra's sang loud and clear. She paused and looked at the clear blue sky. In the face of all this beauty, and with the strains of a love song ringing in her ears, it was almost impossible to believe there was a war raging. Yet here she was, charging right into it.

As Frankie continued to croon about fools rushing in where angels were afraid to go, she shook her head. Was she a fool to live this kind of life, to chase these dreams? This was a dangerous game she was playing.

But if she hadn't been so foolhardy, Fister would have

accomplished his task, and Roosevelt and Churchill would be dead. And though she might have lost Reese, she did save her sister. And now she knew the truth about Reggie Fister.

No, Helen Meeker was no fool. And her "rushing in" had paid off. She was born to do this. And she would keep trying to save the world as long as she had breath in her body.

Feeling good about herself and the mission, she looked at her sister, who was staring at her, no doubt wondering why she hadn't gotten into the car yet.

Suddenly, two gunshots rang out. One bullet exploded through the windshield and buried itself in the cushion on the driver's seat. The second slammed into Meeker's chest, the impact pushing her into the sedan's massive grill.

For a second, she clawed at the hood, looking into Alison's bewildered face. As the strength oozed from her body, she slid down to the pavement. Her mind sank into a dark, deep, black pool.

ACE COLLINS

The President's Service Series

CPSIA information can be obtained at www.ICGtesting.com
Printed in the USA
BVOW03s1037020515

398706BV00013B/246/P